what is chasing the adventurer through the forest?

What else is lurking behind the closet door?

What can you see in the distance?

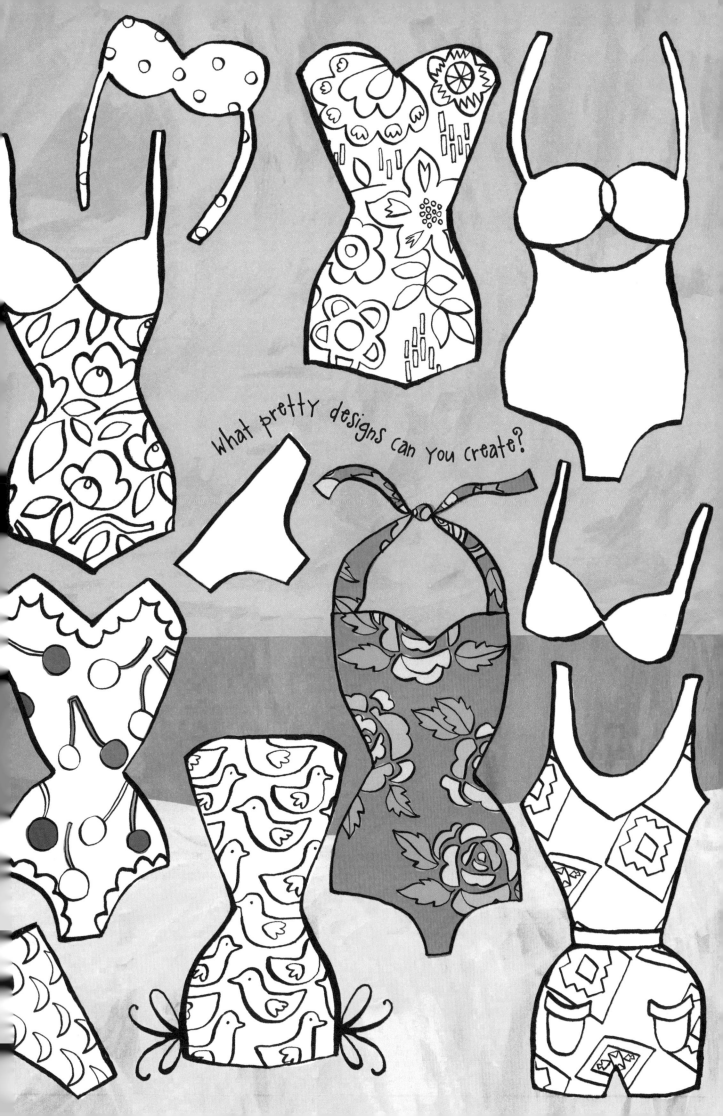

what pretty designs can you create?

what characters can you create out of these household items?

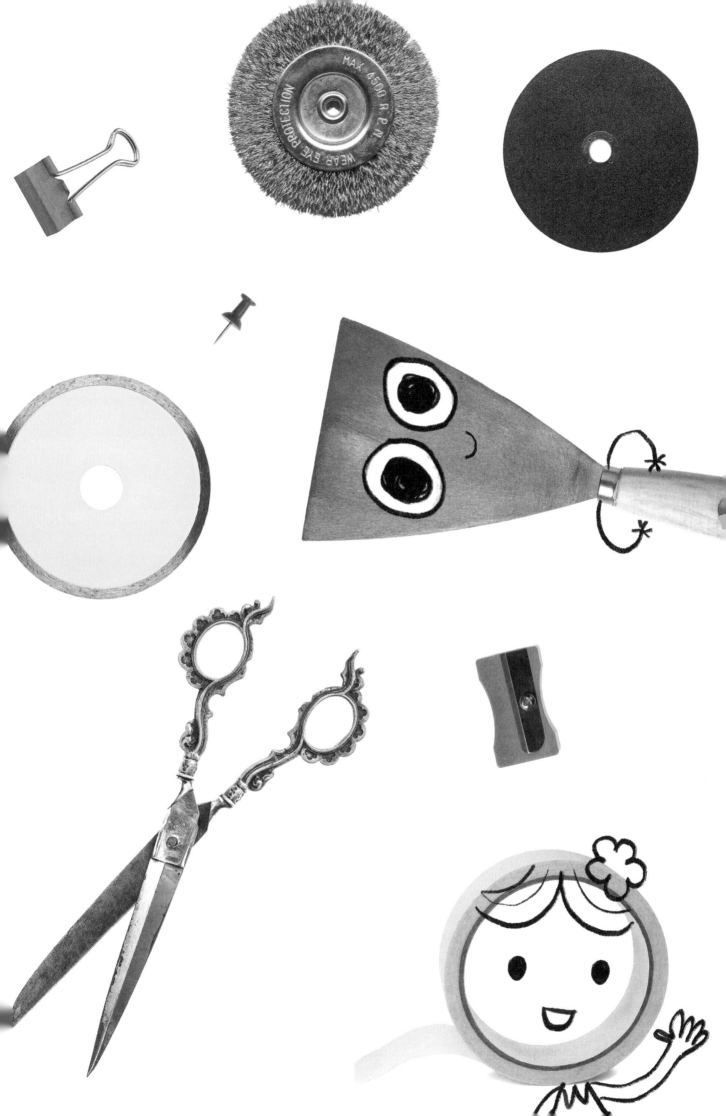

What colours and patterns can you add to the carousel?

What is the street artist drawing on the wall?

What work of art can you create on the canvas?

What presents are in the Christmas stockings?

What is playing at the drive-in?

What sorts of creatures can you turn these handprints into?

What patterns and colours can you add to this Greek Island village?

What kinds of flowers can you create from these buttons?

What varmint is wanted dead or alive?

WANTED

DEAD OR ALIVE
REWARD

What crazy animal portraits are hanging on the wall?

what kinds of hats are the girls wearing?

What awesome designs are on your surfboards?

What is everyone looking at under the bridge?

What kooky characters can you create out of these coins?

What colours are the pigs' clothes?

What's reflected in the mirror?

What else is swimming in the aquarium?

What designs can you add to the buildings?

what is in the pond?

What is going on in the forest outside the photo?

what do the aliens look like in these ufos?

what is happening inside the space station?

TOYS

What has naughty Timmy been scribbling on these photos?

what is the stone gargoyle looking at in the sky above the city?

What decorations can you add to these masks?

ROUND **2**

what is going on in the ocean outside the photo?

What colours do the teams wear in your soccer league?

What do you get when you colour this page and then fold it?

A ▶   Fold back so 'B' meets 'A'   ◀ B

what is reflected in these crazy mirrors and who is making the reflections?

what patterns and colours can you add to the elephants?

What spectacular facial hair can you add to these gentlemen?

What do these zany peoples' shadows look like?

what can you add to these instruments?

What is happening in this street?

Mythical Creatures

What creatures of myth and legend can you create and name?

Pegasus

What can you add to the scrapbook?

SKETCH WHAT?

Published by Hinkler Books Pty Ltd
45–55 Fairchild Street
Heatherton Victoria 3202 Australia
www.hinkler.com.au

© Hinkler Books Pty Ltd 2014

Cover design: Sam Grimmer

Illustrations: Kelly Canby, Smiljana Coh, Louise Cunningham, Woody Fox, Jess Golden, Julie Ingham, Patricia MacCarthy and Keith Robinson

Prepress: Graphic Print Group

All rights reserved. No part of this publication may be reproduced, stored in a retrieval system, or transmitted in any way or by any means, electronic, mechanical, photocopying, recording or otherwise, without the prior written permission of Hinkler Books Pty Ltd.

ISBN: 978 1 7436 3049 5

Printed and bound in China

Images © Shutterstock.com: Open photo album © secondcorner; Vintage portrait two kids © LiliGraphie; Antique family portrait, Antique photo of mother & daughter, Old photograph of three children © Donna Beeler; Twin boys 1890, Two children 1880 © Robert Brown Stock; Brothers antique photo © Susan Law Cain; 1900 vintage photo of family © chippix; Sewing buttons background © manfeiyang; Two wooden buttons © antkevyv; Pink and red buttons © Dejan Dundjerski; Various sewing buttons © donatas1205; Flying disk © Tatiana Popova; Flying disc © cretolamna; Coral garden with starfish and colorful tropical fish © Vilainecrevette; Old log cabin home in Cades Cove © George Allen Penton; Alley at Spittelberg © mradlgruber; Torn piece of white paper with ripped edges © Nicemonkey; Texture of wood background closeup © PinkBlue; Standing griffin with lifted paw © Kristina Birukova; Vector Coloring / Marker Pens (Set 1 of 4) © Diamond_Images; Plastic Marker pen with cap off © Trinacria Photo.